The POWER of PIGGIE BEAR

MARA JAMES
Illustrated By MATTHEW MEW

BROWN BOOKS KIDS

The Power of Piggie Bear®

Brown Books Kids
Dallas / New York
www.BrownBooksKids.com
(972) 381-0009

A New Era in Publishing®

Publisher's Cataloging-In-Publication Data

Names: James, Mara, author. | Mew, Matt, illustrator.
Title: The power of Piggie Bear / Mara James ; illustrated by Matthew Mew.
Description: Dallas ; New York : Brown Books Kids, [2021] | Interest age level: 003-005. | Summary: "Piggie
    Bear is here to teach young children all about how special they are, how to identify their own feelings,
    and then how to handle and manage those feelings. Piggie Bear knows that sometimes emotions can be
    overwhelming for someone so small, and that learning healthy emotional practices is very important for
    growing up happy and healthy"--Provided by publisher.
Identifiers: ISBN 9781612545028
Subjects: LCSH: Self-esteem--Juvenile fiction. | Emotions--Juvenile fiction. | Stuffed animals (Toys)--Juvenile
    fiction. | CYAC: Self-esteem--Fiction. | Emotions--Fiction. | Stuffed animals (Toys)--Fiction.
Classification: LCC PZ7.1.J38536 Po 2021 | DDC [E]--dc23

This book has been officially leveled by using the F&P Text Level Gradient™ Leveling System.

ISBN 978-1-61254-502-8
LCCN 2020917905

Printed in China
10 9 8 7 6 5 4 3 2 1

For more information or to contact the author, please go to
www.ELFempowers.org.

Piggie Bear is owned by the Extraordinary Lives Foundation, a 501(c)(3)
whose mission is to improve children's mental health & wellness.

Dedication

This book is dedicated to children
around the world. May their hearts be
filled with love, light, and happiness.

Acknowledgments

We would like to thank all of the people who helped
bring Piggie Bear to life, including Dr. Kenneth James,
the Extraordinary Lives Foundation, and Brown Books
Publishing. We're so glad you believe in the power of
Piggie Bear. You are all amazing!

Hi, I'm Piggie Bear!
What's your name?

It's so nice to meet you.

Let's play peekaboo! I see you.

I'm not in the MIDDLE.

I'm not up HIGH.

I'm not GREEN or BROWN

or the color of the SKY.

Can you find me sitting on the shelf?

When I am picked up from the
shelf and given big, warm hugs,
it makes me feel really HAPPY!

Can you show me your happy face?

Some people think that I look like a PIG.

Some people think that I look like a BEAR.

It doesn't matter what we look like.
We are all AMAZING just the way we are!

I would like to share my favorite Piggie Bear saying with you.

Are you ready? Open your arms out wide, with your hands facing the sky. Repeat after me:

"I AM AMAZING!"

YOU ARE AMAZING!

Don't ever forget how
truly wonderful you are.

But there are some days
when I don't feel so amazing.

There are days when I feel
angry, worried, or frustrated.

I call these my
GRUMPY, BUMPY, LUMPY days.

Do you ever feel this way?

ANGRY

WORRIED

FRUSTRATED

Do you know what I do to help me feel better? I practice my special Piggie Bear breathing.

Would you like to learn how to do this?

Put your hands on your belly. Breathe in through your nose. Feel your belly grow

BIGGER.

Now, blow the air out through your mouth. Feel your belly grow **SMALL**ᴇʀ.

Keep your hands on your belly.
Breathe in through your nose.
Do you feel your belly grow

BIGGER?

Now, blow the air out
through your mouth. Do
you feel your belly grow

SMALLER?

GREAT JOB!

There are other days when I feel sad, lonely, or scared.

I call these my
FoOZY, WOOZY, DOOZY days.

Do you ever feel this way?

SAD

LONELY

SCARED

Everyone has feelings like these,
EVEN ME!

I would like to share my favorite Piggie Bear hug with you. I do it whenever I am feeling this way.

ARE YOU READY?

Cross your arms around your shoulders and give yourself a big hug. AHHHH!

My special Piggie Bear hug makes
me feel warm and fuzzy inside.
This makes me feel better.

I hope that it makes you feel better too!

Before I go, let's play a game together. Put your hand on your heart and feel it go bump.

Ba-bump!

Ba-bump!

Ba-bump!

Now repeat after me:

"In my heart
I can see
Piggie Bear smiling

HAPPILY! "

About the Author

Originally from New York, Mara James relocated to California with her husband and her three children in 2007. They established Dr. James's OBGYN practice, and for seven years, Mara managed the busy office. Then, in 2014, Mara unexpectedly experienced a manic episode and was diagnosed with bipolar disorder.

Through her battle with mental health, many wellness professionals helped Mara heal and transform her life. Mara's experience—in addition to the experience of some of her close family members—has kindled in her a passion for forwarding the cause of children's mental health. She established the Extraordinary Lives Foundation and created Piggie Bear to promote mental health awareness and provide both children and their parents with the resources they need to pursue holistic wellness in any and all avenues available.

Mara lives with her family in Orange County, California.

About the Illustrator

Matthew Mew has been working with children's books and materials as an author and illustrator for over thirty-five years. After graduating from UCLA with a degree in design, he worked for six years as a character illustrator in the Disneyland Creative Services Department. For the past thirty years he has been a freelancer, designing and illustrating children's products and print media for companies both large and small.